Hayley
the Rain
Fairy

To Alexandra 'Tink' Gunn
– a very special girl

Special thanks to
Sue Bentley

ISBN-10: 0-439-81392-1
ISBN-13: 978-0-439-81392-1

12 11 10 9 8 7 6 5 4 3 2 1   9 10 11 12/0

Printed in the U.S.A.   40

First Scholastic printing, March 2007

Hayley
the Rain
Fairy

by Daisy Meadows
illustrated by Georgie Ripper

A
LITTLE APPLE
PAPERBACK

SCHOLASTIC INC.

New York Toronto London Auckland Sydney
Mexico City New Delhi Hong Kong Buenos Aires

The
Fairyland
Palace

Forest o

Candy Factory

The
Village
Hall

River

Wetherbury Village

Far

Jack Frost's
Ice Castle

Green Wood

Mrs. Fordham's House

The Park

Willow Hill

High St.

The Museum

Kirsty's House

Fields

Mudhole

N
W E
S

Goblins green and goblins small,
I cast this spell to make you tall.
As high as the palace you shall grow.
My icy magic makes it so.

Then steal the rooster's magic feathers,
used by the fairies to make all weathers.
Climate chaos I have planned
on Earth, and here, in Fairyland!

Contents

Water, Water Everywhere!

"OK, OK, I'm awake. You can stop ringing now," mumbled Kirsty Tate sleepily. She reached out to turn off her alarm clock. But strangely, the alarm wasn't ringing.

Quack, quack, quack! The noise that had woken her rang through the air again.

Now that Kirsty was awake, she

realized that the sound hadn't been
coming from her alarm clock at all. It
was coming from outside instead. She
jumped out of bed and peeked out
through the curtains. "Oh!" she cried.
There was water rising right up to her
windowsill. A large brown duck was
swimming past, followed by five fluffy
ducklings! Kirsty watched as the mother
duck fussed over her babies.

It had been
raining really hard
all night. In the
front yard,
the grass and
flowerbeds had
flooded. Water
lapped against the
walls of the old barn,
and out past the front
gate the street looked
like a silvery mirror.

Kirsty rushed over to her best friend,
Rachel Walker, who was asleep in the
guest bed. Rachel was staying with
Kirsty for a week during her summer
vacation. "Wake up, Rachel! You have
to see this!" Kirsty said, shaking her
friend gently.

Rachel sat up and rubbed her eyes.
"What's going on?"

"I think the river must have
overflowed. Everything in Wetherbury is
flooded!" replied Kirsty.

"Really?" Rachel was wide awake
now, eagerly looking out the window.
"That's odd," she said, pointing. "The
water isn't that deep in the front yard
and the street. How can it be right up to
your bedroom window at the same
time?"

"Maybe it's Weather Fairy magic!" Kirsty gasped, her eyes shining.

"Of course!" Rachel agreed. She knew that fairy magic followed its own rules.

Kirsty and Rachel were special friends of the fairies. The two girls had met while on vacation with their parents on Rainspell Island. There, they had helped the seven Rainbow Fairies get home to Fairyland after Jack Frost's spell had cast them out. Now Jack Frost was up to more trouble, and Rachel and Kirsty were on another secret fairy mission, this time with the Weather Fairies.

Rachel looked over at Doodle, the weather vane on top of the barn. Usually, with the help of the Weather Fairies, Doodle the rooster was in charge of the weather in Fairyland. Each of his seven magic tail feathers controlled a different type of weather. But Jack Frost had sent his goblins to steal these magic feathers, and they had run away with them into the human world. Doodle had followed, but without his feathers, and outside of Fairyland, he had transformed into an ordinary metal weather vane.

Kirsty's dad had found him lying in the park and brought him home. That's where he would have to stay until Kirsty and Rachel could return all seven of his tail feathers and send him back to Fairyland. They had already found six feathers, so there was just one more left to find!

"Today's the last day of my vacation," Rachel said sadly.

"I know! We have to find the magic Rain Feather today," Kirsty called over her shoulder as she quickly got dressed. "It's our last chance. At least with all this magical flooding, we can be sure that the goblin who stole the feather isn't far away!"

Just then, there was a tapping noise at the window. "What if that's the goblin?" Rachel whispered nervously. The goblins were mean, and Jack Frost had cast a spell to make them even bigger than usual. There was a rule in Fairyland that nothing could be taller than the highest tower of the fairy palace, but the goblins were still pretty big. They reached up to the girls' shoulders!

Kirsty put her finger to her lips. "Shh," she warned, edging toward the window. She peeked out, then threw

back the curtains with a smile. An elegant white swan was tapping on the window with its beak. And a tiny fairy was sitting on the swan's back, waving at the girls.

"Oh!" Rachel gasped in delight. "It's Hayley the Rain Fairy!"

Goblin Afloat

Kirsty was just about to open the window to let Hayley in, but then she hesitated. "All of the water will rush inside," she said, frowning.

Hayley laughed. It sounded like a tinkling bell. "Don't worry!" she called through the window. "It's fairy rain. It doesn't spill into people's houses."

Slowly, Kirsty opened the window. The water stayed right where it was!

Rachel leaned forward. She could tell that a strange invisible barrier was holding the water back. "It feels like jelly!" she said, poking her finger into it. The water on the other side of the barrier felt just like normal. Hayley fluttered through the window and blew the swan a kiss. "Thanks for the ride!" she said. "Good-bye!" The swan dipped its head and glided away. "Hello, girls," Hayley sang happily.

"Hello again, Hayley," Kirsty replied. She and Rachel had met Hayley in Fairyland at the beginning of their adventure, along with all of the other Weather Fairies.

"We're so glad to see you," added Rachel.

Hayley hovered in the air. She wore a pretty violet skirt and a matching top. Her long, dark hair was tied up in a ponytail and decorated with a bright blue flower. She folded her arms, and little droplets of blue and violet scattered from her silver wand. "It's time to get Doodle's Rain Feather back from that terrible goblin!" she said firmly, eyes flashing.

"We think so, too," Rachel agreed. "But how can we look for him with all this flooding? We really need a boat."

That gave Kirsty an idea. "I helped Dad clean out the garage last week, and we found an old raft. Let's go ask if we can take it out to play."

Hayley dived off the curtain rail, her delicate wings flashing, and landed on Rachel's shoulder. She hid beneath Rachel's hair.

The girls found Mr. and Mrs. Tate in the kitchen. Mr. Tate looked baffled as

he stared out of the window. "Since I can't get to work in this rain, I think I'll work on a mathematical theory about this flood water . . ." he murmured, wandering past them.

"Hello, girls," said Mrs. Tate with a smile. "Your dad's trying to figure out why the water isn't flooding into the house, Kirsty. But I'm just glad the place is dry! I made some toast. Help yourselves."

"Thanks, Mom." Kirsty grabbed a piece of toast. "Is it OK if we go out in the old raft?"

Mrs. Tate smiled. "Sounds fine to me. Just be careful, please!"

Kirsty and Rachel rushed out to the garage, finishing their toast on the way.

Kirsty pulled out the raft, along with an air pump and two wooden paddles. It didn't take long to inflate the raft. Then the girls pushed it out through the window of the garage, onto the water. They climbed in carefully. It was just big enough for two people.

"Perfect!" said Hayley. She fluttered down to the front of the raft, where she sat like a tiny sparkling figurehead. Blue and violet droplets scattered from her wand.

"Here we go!" Rachel dipped her paddle into the water.

Kirsty began paddling, too. At first, the raft spun in circles. As the girls got the hang of steering it, they began moving out toward High Street.

Suddenly, a lady in a yellow raincoat and boots jumped out in front of them.

"Look out, Kirsty! It's the crossing

guard!" called Rachel. She dragged her
paddle in the water, using it as a brake.
Quick as a flash, Hayley whooshed into
Kirsty's pocket, out of sight.

"Let the people cross!" said the crossing
guard, holding out her arms.

Kirsty and Rachel waited for a man
to cross the street. He was pulling a
floating wooden box with a dog sitting
inside.

"Thank you. All clear!" The crossing

guard smiled at Rachel and Kirsty as
they paddled on.

Outside the post office, the girls saw a
group of kids splashing about happily.
They all wore boots and raincoats and
didn't seem to mind the pouring rain at
all. But not everyone was enjoying the
rain. Kirsty spotted a cat perched in an
oak tree in the village square. "Poor
thing," she said. "At least it's safe up
there."

As they continued paddling toward the park, Rachel saw a strange, dark shape floating out from behind the playground slide. "Look over there. It's an upside-down umbrella!" she cried, pointing.

Kirsty's eyes widened. Four ducks, all connected to some sort of rope, were quacking loudly, and pulling an umbrella

boat along. Inside sat a hunched, dripping wet figure.

Suddenly, Rachel realized who it was. "It's the goblin," she gasped. "And he could spot us at any moment!"

Stop, Thief!

"Quick, hide!" Hayley whispered. "We need to come up with a plan."

Kirsty and Rachel looked around desperately. The goblin was coming closer and closer. There was nowhere to hide!

"What about the trees?" Kirsty suggested. "If we turn into fairies, we can hide in the branches!"

Rachel pulled out the magic locket that the Fairy Queen had given her to use in times of danger. Kirsty found hers, too, and both girls sprinkled themselves with glittering fairy dust. Kirsty felt her shoulders tingle as delicate fairy wings grew there. She fluttered straight into the air, heading for the nearest branch.

Rachel also felt herself shrinking. She zoomed upward on her sparkly wings and landed next to Kirsty. Just then, she spotted an empty bird's nest

on a nearby branch. "Quick! In here!"
she whispered.

Kirsty and Hayley jumped in beside
Rachel. The nest was lined
with moss and fluffy
feathers. It felt cozy and dry.
"Great idea, Rachel. This is
a perfect place to
hide!" Hayley said,
grinning.

As soon as the
girls were out of
sight, the goblin
floated beneath the tree in
his umbrella boat. One of
the ducks flapped its wings angrily,
pulling at its rope. The umbrella wobbled
in the water and almost tipped over.

"Hey! I almost fell out!" the goblin
complained. "Stop trying to get away,
you silly ducks. You've got my nice
warm scarf for a rope. I'm the one who's
freezing! *Achoo*!" His loud sneeze echoed
through the park like a foghorn.

Kirsty, Rachel, and Hayley quietly
peeked out of the nest. They could see

that the goblin was very thin, with enormous hands and feet. Rain poured from the brim of his battered hat and dripped onto his long, crooked nose.

The goblin shivered and sniffed. He rubbed the tip of his nose, which was all red and shiny. "It's not fair. I wanted to go after the Sunshine Feather, and instead I get stuck with this rotten old Rain Feather! I should be toasty warm, not as cold as yesterday's mud oatmeal and as soggy as a squashed worm! *Achoo!*"

"He has a really nasty cold," murmured Hayley.

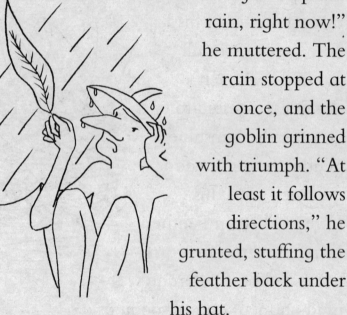

"Serves him right!" Kirsty said. Just then, the goblin lifted his hat and pulled out a beautiful copper-colored feather with silvery streaks. He jabbed it angrily into the air. "Just stop this rain, right now!" he muttered. The rain stopped at once, and the goblin grinned with triumph. "At least it follows directions," he grunted, stuffing the feather back under his hat.

"Oh, the poor Rain Feather!" whispered Hayley.

Suddenly, the goblin's miserable face lit up with a grin. He had spotted the girls' raft. "Oh, goody, a real boat just for me!" he cried. Using his big hands as paddles, the goblin pulled up alongside the raft. Then he scrunched up his long legs, sprang straight in the air, and landed in the raft. "Nice duckies. Let's harness you to my new boat," he said. "That's it. All ready now. Off we go!"

"That awful goblin! He's stealing our raft!" Kirsty explained. "And now he's using the umbrella to keep himself dry."

"I feel like some more rain now!" shouted the goblin happily. He took out the Rain Feather and waved it in the air. A big, gray cloud appeared above the trees. Rain began to pour down. "Faster, ducks! Swim faster!"

urged the goblin, his voice growing
fainter as the raft sailed out of sight.

Rachel, Kirsty, and Hayley watched in
dismay. "How are we going to get the
Rain Feather back now?" Rachel asked,
sighing.

Feathered Friends

Kirsty stood up. "I have a plan!" she announced.

"Hooray! What is it?" Hayley asked.

"Remember how the goblin said he had wanted the Sunshine Feather?" Kirsty began.

Hayley and Rachel both nodded.

"Well, if we could find a feather that

looks like the Sunshine Feather, then we might be able to trick the goblin into swapping with us!" explained Kirsty.

"It's a good plan. But where can we get a feather?" Rachel wondered. "The magic feathers are so long and beautiful."

Kirsty grinned and flew into the air. "Follow me!"

Hayley and Rachel zoomed after Kirsty. She led them back over toward her house and then to the nearby farmyard. The farmhouse and cow shed were flooded with a few inches of water.

Kirsty swooped through the henhouse door with Hayley and Rachel close behind. Inside, they saw fluffy, dark shapes huddled together on a perch above the wet floor.

"Excuse me," Hayley said politely to the chickens. "We need your help."

The chickens looked up with dull eyes. "Eggs all wet. Feet cold and muddy. Feathers all soggy," they squawked sadly.

"Oh, dear. They seem so upset," Hayley said with a sigh.

"It's because everything is so wet. Dad says chickens really hate being soggy," Kirsty explained.

Hayley flew down to pet the chickens' heads. "Don't worry, chickens. We can make this rain stop with your help," she told them brightly.

"We need a big feather, as long as this —"
Kirsty said, spreading out her hands to show what she meant.

"Why didn't you say so?" squawked a handsome rooster. He twisted around and plucked a feather from his tail. "Will this do?"

"Oh, yes! It's beautiful. Thank you
very much." Hayley fluttered down
and took the feather. "Now, cheer up!"
she said, flying toward the door.
"We're going to go stop
the rain!"

"Thank you," called Kirsty
and Rachel as they followed
Hayley to the door.

The chickens fluffed
themselves up,
already looking
much happier. They
lifted their wings to
wave at the girls.
"Good-bye!" they clucked.

Outside, on the henhouse roof, Hayley,
Rachel, and Kirsty looked at the long
copper-colored feather. "I don't think the

goblin will be fooled," Hayley said
doubtfully. "The Sunshine Feather is
covered with golden yellow spots."

Kirsty grinned. "No problem. There's a
can of yellow paint in our garage!"

They all rushed back to the garage.
Inside, Kirsty struggled to open the paint
can. "The lid's stuck!" she groaned.

Hayley tapped the can with her wand,
and a shower of sparkles twinkled around
the lid. It popped right open! Moments
later, Kirsty had painted tiny yellow
speckles on the feather.

"Perfect! It looks just like the Sunshine Feather!" exclaimed Hayley.

"Now all we have to do is find the goblin," said Rachel.

Just then, a group of ducks flew by. Without a word, Hayley rose up in a cloud of violet sparkles. Rachel and Kirsty watched her, a tiny spot of light, as she flew next to the ducks in the rain.

Before long, she was back and she had news for the girls. "The ducks just saw the goblin in the field behind the museum!" Hayley declared. "Let's go!"

The girls followed Hayley to the back of the museum. Sure enough, there was the goblin, floating across the flooded field in Kirsty's raft. "*Achoo!*" he sputtered loudly. "I'm sick of being wet and miserable. And my cold's getting worse."

Hayley, Kirsty, and Rachel floated at a safe distance from the goblin. "Here goes," Hayley said bravely. "I have something you might like," she called to

the goblin in a
singsong voice, waving
the fake Sunshine
Feather.

The goblin's eyes
lit up greedily.
"The Sunshine
Feather! Give it to
me!" His long arm
shot out and his fat
fingers grabbed for the
feather, but Hayley was
too quick for him. She sped backward
out of his reach. "Oh, rats! Almost had
two magic feathers!" said the goblin,
scowling.

Hayley drifted forward again. "I'll
trade my feather for yours, if you like,"
she offered sweetly. Rachel and Kirsty

held their breath. Would the goblin fall
for their trick?

"OK," the goblin said right away.
"Anything for some warmth. Now, give
it to me!" Hayley zoomed down and
grabbed the Rain Feather,
thrusting the pretend
Sunshine Feather
at the goblin.
He grabbed
it and stroked it
fondly with a wide
grin on his face.
Hayley immediately
waved the Rain
Feather in a complicated pattern.
"Rain, stop!" she ordered.
The rain stopped at once. The gray
clouds melted away, and steam rose as

the floodwater began to dry up. Then the
sun came out, turning the shallow pools
and puddles golden.

The goblin waved his feather
triumphantly. "My Sunshine Feather's
working already!" he boasted. "I'm
leaving now. It's about time I took a

vacation." He leaped out of the raft and splashed away across the field.

Rachel, Kirsty, and Hayley hugged one another happily. "We did it!" Kirsty exclaimed.

"Yes, and now we've found all seven magic feathers!" cried Rachel.

"We can return the Rain Feather to Doodle, and he can take charge of Fairyland's weather again," said Hayley.

She did a happy cartwheel in the air.
Violet and blue sparks fizzed around her.

Kirsty was about to turn toward home,
when she suddenly shivered. "That's
strange. It's getting really cold," she said.

Rachel looked at her in alarm. "Oh,
no! Remember Doodle's warning? He
said 'Beware! Jack Frost will come if his
goblins fail!'" There was a crackling
noise as the floodwater stopped draining
away and began to freeze.

Hayley paled. "It is Jack Frost," she
squealed. "He's coming!"

Frost Fright

A tall, bony figure, dressed all in white, suddenly appeared out of thin air. Icicles hung from his eyebrows and beard. "You again!" he snarled at Kirsty and Rachel. "How dare you steal those feathers?"

Rachel, Kirsty, and Hayley gasped in fear as Jack Frost towered over them.

Kirsty looked at Hayley. "Go!" she

whispered. "Take the Rain Feather to
Doodle before Jack Frost gets his hands
on it."

Hayley looked unsure, but she
nodded and zoomed away, violet fairy
dust streaming out behind her like a
comet's tail.

"As for you, you useless goblin!" Jack Frost was saying. "I'll send you on a vacation you won't forget!" He lifted his wand and blasted freezing white light toward the goblin, who was stomping away across the field. With a fizz and a crackle, the goblin became a skinny ice statue!

Jack Frost turned back to face the girls. He shrieked with rage when he saw that Hayley had left. He glared at Kirsty, who was reaching for her locket. "No, you don't!" he snapped. He pointed his

wand and a narrow beam of light shot out, freezing both lockets tightly shut.

"Oh!" cried Rachel and Kirsty. Without their fairy dust, they would be fairy-sized forever! Jack Frost looked down at the two tiny girls. "What's the matter? Are your tongues frozen?" he asked, laughing noisily. His laughter sounded like feet crunching on snail shells.

Kirsty trembled with fright, but she looked straight into Jack Frost's cold, gray eyes. "Why can't you live in peace with all the other fairies?" she asked.

"Fairyland is a wonderful place!

Everyone would be your friend if you stopped causing so much trouble," Rachel added.

Jack Frost's mouth tightened with surprise. He seemed speechless. For a moment, Rachel and Kirsty wondered if he would listen to them. Then Kirsty's heart sank as Jack Frost frowned.

"How dare you give me advice?" he roared, his eyes as cold as a glacier. "You two have interfered too many times. I think it's time I put a stop to that!" He raised his wand.

Rachel grabbed Kirsty's arm and pulled
her behind a nearby tree, just as a blast of
freezing white light poured out of the
wand. There was a loud snapping sound,
and thick white ice coated the tree.

Kirsty and Rachel shivered. Jack Frost stepped around the tree and raised his wand again. Rachel heard a rushing sound and squeezed her eyes shut, expecting to feel an icy blast at any moment. . . .

Rainbow's End

But, instead, Rachel heard Jack Frost give a scream of rage. She opened her eyes.

Doodle, the fairy rooster, flew up in a great rush of wind and fire. His magnificent tail glittered with sparks of red and gold and copper. "Get away from them, Jack Frost!" he ordered, his beak snapping with anger. He flapped his wings furiously. A stream of white-hot sparks sprayed from them and sizzled on the ice.

"Ouch! Stop that!" cried Jack Frost, backing away as several sparks landed on his robe. Little puffs of steam leaked from his spiky hair and beard.

"Doodle's come to save us!" breathed Kirsty. "And he's his true magical self again!"

Hayley flew over to
the girls. "Are you all
right? You're so brave
to face Jack Frost
when you were
only fairy-sized."

"We had to. He
froze our magic
lockets shut," Rachel
told her.

Keeping one fierce amber eye on Jack
Frost, Doodle came over and swept
Rachel, Kirsty, and Hayley under one
wing. Then he peered down his beak at
Jack Frost. "You must pay for what
you've done!" he said severely. "Not
only have you created trouble with the
weather, but you have threatened two of
Fairyland's dearest friends!"

Jack Frost cowered. Melting ice ran down his face and dripped from his sharp nose. "They shouldn't have stuck their noses into my business," he snapped.

"What if Jack Frost casts a spell on Doodle?" Rachel asked anxiously.

Hayley shook her head. "Now that he has all his feathers back, Doodle is seven times as powerful as any one fairy. He's more than a match for Jack Frost!"

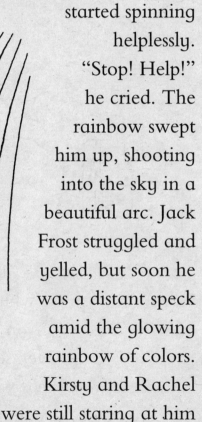

Doodle fluttered his magic tail feathers.
Colored sparks shot out, and a
rainbow began rising from
the ground. Jack Frost
started spinning
helplessly.
"Stop! Help!"
he cried. The
rainbow swept
him up, shooting
into the sky in a
beautiful arc. Jack
Frost struggled and
yelled, but soon he
was a distant speck
amid the glowing
rainbow of colors.
Kirsty and Rachel
were still staring at him

when they felt themselves being whisked
up in a whirlwind of shimmering fairy
dust. With Hayley and Doodle, the girls
sped through the bright blue sky. Soft
feathers floated
around them and
they could smell
sweet summer
flowers in the air.
"Oh," breathed
Rachel happily.
She caught a
glimpse of green
fields and red-and-
white toadstool houses
on the ground below.
Then some clouds parted,
and there were the towers of the beautiful
fairy palace, gleaming in the sunshine!

"It's Fairyland! And look, the weather's still mixed up!" called Kirsty.

A crowd of fairies waved and cheered as Doodle and the girls landed in the courtyard of the fairy palace. King Oberon and Queen Titania were waiting to greet them.

"Welcome back, Doodle. We have missed our weather rooster," said the King and Queen warmly. "And our heartfelt thanks to you, Rachel and Kirsty."

All the people of Fairyland cheered again. The Weather Fairies gathered happily around Doodle, eager to get back to their weather work.

"What's going to happen to Jack Frost, Your Majesties?" Kirsty asked.

Titania looked stern. "He will stay at the end of the rainbow until he sees the error of his ways. He's gone too far this time," she said.

Kirsty and Rachel smiled with relief.
*That should keep him out of mischief for a
while*, Rachel thought. "We'd better give
back our magic
lockets," she
said to Kirsty.

Oberon shook
his head. "You
must keep them,
my dears." He
waved his hand
over the lockets.
Silver sparkles shot

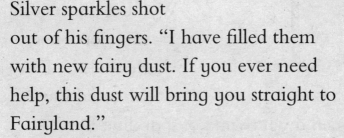

out of his fingers. "I have filled them
with new fairy dust. If you ever need
help, this dust will bring you straight to
Fairyland."

"Where you will always be welcome,"
added Titania with a sweet smile.

Kirsty and Rachel's eyes opened wide. This was a great honor!

Then Doodle came forward. "I have a gift for you, too," he said, and gave them a weather vane that looked just like him. "Oh! Thank you all so much," said the girls. They hugged each of the Weather Fairies and said good-bye to Doodle and the Fairy King and Queen.

Then a whirlwind of sparkling fairy dust swept them upward. In a few moments, they landed back in Kirsty's yard.

Kirsty's dad appeared from behind the barn, looking puzzled. "Oh, you found that old weather vane. I've been looking for it everywhere. Where was it?"

"It appeared by magic," Kirsty told him, her eyes sparkling. Rachel smiled.

Mr. Tate laughed, scratching his head. "Well, I'd better put it back. I've gotten used to seeing it up there."

"Me, too," Kirsty agreed.

Just as Mr. Tate was putting the weather vane up on the barn, a car pulled into the driveway.

"It's my mom and dad!" Rachel said, waving.

"Hello, you two. Have you had a good week?" asked Mr. and Mrs. Walker as they climbed out of the car.

"The best! It's been really magical!" Rachel replied, hugging her parents.

The girls went upstairs to get Rachel's things together, while their parents had tea in the kitchen. Then it was time for Rachel to leave. Kirsty hugged her friend good-bye.

"You must come and visit *us* soon," Mrs. Walker said to Kirsty.

"Yes, soon!" Rachel added.

"I'd love to, thanks," Kirsty smiled. "Good-bye, Rachel. I'll see you on our next vacation!"

After Rachel had left, Kirsty stood in
the yard thinking about all of their
adventures. She looked up at the barn
roof. For a moment, a shining rainbow
touched the old tiles and the weather
vane spun around swiftly. As it did,
Kirsty could have sworn she saw the
rooster wink at her and sparkle with fairy
magic.

THIS LITTLE RASCAL NEEDS A HOME!

THE **PUPPY PLACE**

Where every puppy finds a home

RASCAL

ELLEN MILES

📖SCHOLASTIC

RASCAL IS THE PETERSONS' NEW FOSTER PUPPY. HE'S A LITTLE JACK RUSSELL TERRIER WHO GETS INTO BIG TROUBLE. LIZZIE AND CHARLES ARE IN FOR A CHALLENGE. WILL THEY BE ABLE TO FIND A HOME FOR THIS PESKY LITTLE PUPPY?

📖SCHOLASTIC

www.scholastic.com